# LITTLE TOOT
## ON THE MISSISSIPPI

*About the Book*

When the Mississippi River goes into flood, adventure-loving Little Toot sets out on a daring rescue mission. The plucky little tugboat, with the help of several forlorn old steamboats, once again faces a challenge to his resourcefulness.

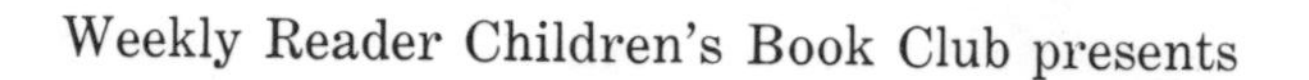
Weekly Reader Children's Book Club presents

# LITTLE TOOT

# ON THE MISSISSIPPI

by HARDIE GRAMATKY

G. P. PUTNAM'S SONS NEW YORK

 Published simultaneously in
Canada by Longman Canada Limited, Toronto.
SBN: GB-399-60853-2
SBN: TR-399-20364-8
Library of Congress Catalog Card Number: 73-76717
PRINTED IN THE UNITED STATES OF AMERICA
06209
Weekly Reader Children's Book Club Edition

Spring came and with it a longing to travel. Little Toot wanted more than anything to go to the Mississippi.

Grandfather Toot had told
him all about that mighty
old river. And he had told
him unbelievable tales about
its steamboats. Great
horned monsters they were!
They chewed fire and breathed
smoke like a dragon!

Strange visions of steamboats
floated through the little
tugboat's head as he set out on

his great adventure. He had no idea of what lay before him or of the troubles that awaited him.

His newly polished
smokestack gleamed
brightly in the sunlight
as Little Toot arrived at the
Mighty Mississippi. He
was so excited that he blew
a joyful blast on his whistle.
But *where were the
steamboats?*

No smoke from fire-eating monsters
could be seen anywhere along
the horizon. No splashing of paddle
wheels could be heard.

Eagerly, Little Toot searched around islands. He hunted among willows and reeds. To be sure, there were alligators, bats, raccoons, and skunks. But, alas, there were no steamboats.

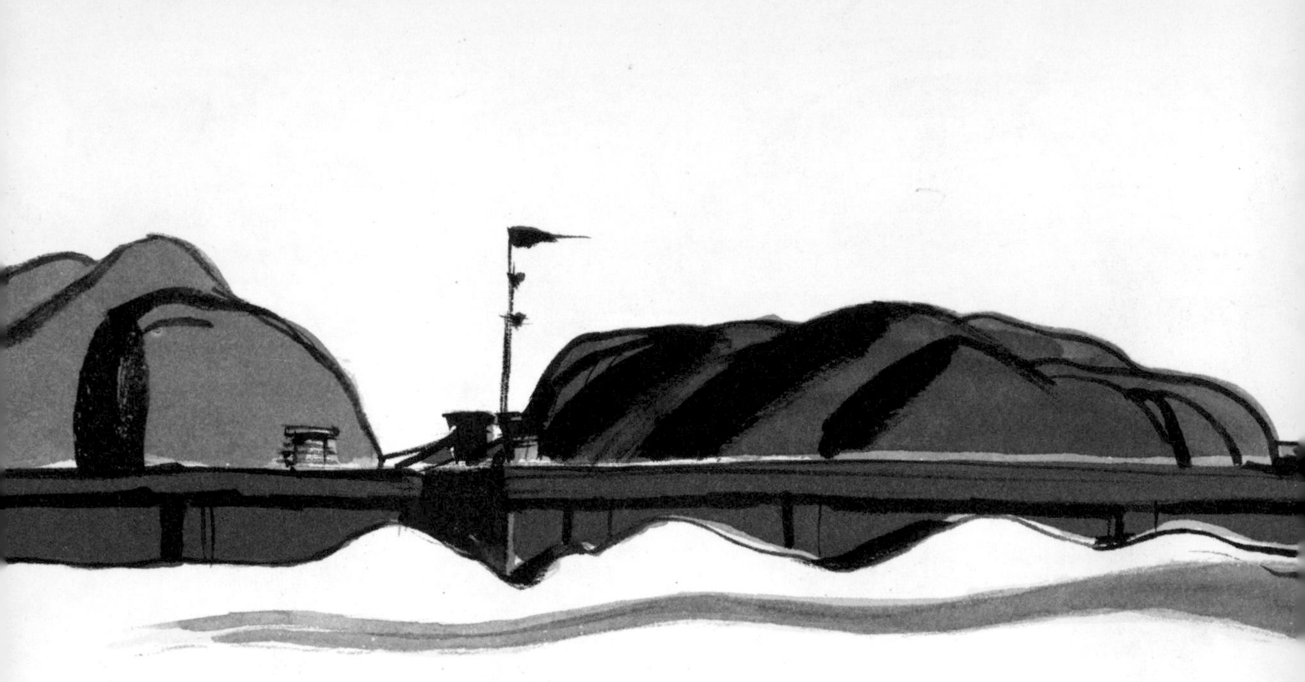

There were towboats, all right—
enormous towboats, thrashing and
pounding their way up the river.
They pushed a string of barges
before them long as a freight
train. And the waves they kicked
up were awful.

"Where are the steamboats?"
asked Little Toot timidly.

"*Steamboats!* What do you mean *steamboats?* We never heard of anything called steamboats," roared one of the towboats.

Then they all laughed at
the little tugboat for having
such a foolish idea.

With an air of importance they went on their way, showering Little Toot with their waves.

"Steamboats are great horned monsters," Little Toot called after them. "They breathe smoke and chew fire like a dragon!"

He felt it his duty to warn them,
but he was only washed up on a snag
for his trouble.

Poor Little Toot!
Stranded there between
sky and water, he wondered
how he would ever get
back down on the river.

Fortunately, a little coalboat
came wandering through the reeds.
"What are you doing up there?"
asked the coalboat.
"I'm looking for steamboats,"
said Little Toot, a bit embarrassed
at his awkward position.

The coalboat was puzzled, but with a heave and a shove, he helped Little Toot down onto the water. "I remember steamboats," said the coalboat wistfully. "But there haven't been any steamboats around for years." "Was the Old Mississippi afraid of steamboats?" asked Little Toot excitedly.

"I can see you don't know
much about the Mississippi,"
said the coalboat. "The Old
River is afraid of nothing.
He is majestic—a king
among rivers. He reaches
out across America, and he
does the land much good.
Most of the time he
is gentle and kind—

"But you had better watch out when
he gets mad!
Rainstorms make the Old River
angry, and when he gets angry,
he goes into flood."

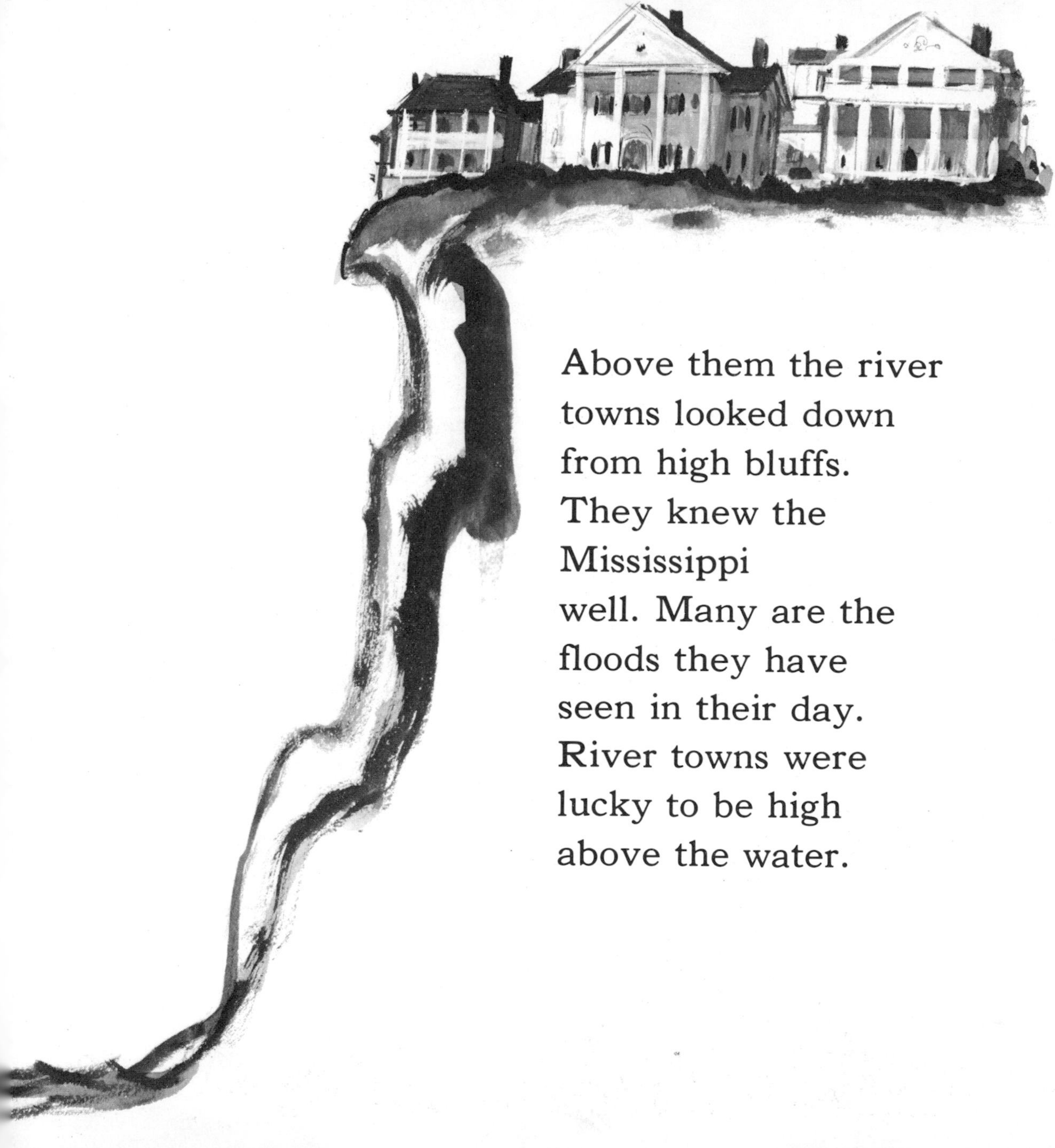

Above them the river
towns looked down
from high bluffs.
They knew the
Mississippi
well. Many are the
floods they have
seen in their day.
River towns were
lucky to be high
above the water.

"But there are some river towns that are not so lucky," said the coalboat. "People live here in the shadow of a levee. The levee is a high wall that protects them from flood."

At that moment a peal of
thunder growled in the
distance. Black storm
clouds gathered overhead,
and deep shadows fell
across the river.

Then the skies
opened, and the rain
poured down.

Gusts of wind rocked the two
boats violently, and waves
slapped angrily at the levee.

Little Toot went wild with fear. He remembered what the coalboat had told him about floods. He was afraid of what the river might do. Frantically, he raced about, looking for a way out.

Lightning flashed as
the little tugboat
slipped through a
narrow opening into an
inlet grown over with
trees.
"Wait!" called the
coalboat. But the
terrified Little Toot
blundered on.

Then he dashed headlong
into a bayou.
The bayou was a dark and
dismal place. Moss
hung down from the
branches of trees, and
roots snagged up out of
the swamp water.
Yet all seemed peaceful
and quiet.

But not for long. Around him there arose a crescendo of howls the like of which he had never heard before. Strange sounds of unseen animals came from deep in the wilderness. Little Toot was scared green.

From where he was Little
Toot saw bright,
gleaming eyes glowing
at him out of the dark.

He was afraid to move. When finally he got up courage, he ran into even more trouble. He ran into a monstrous *thing!*

"Who are you?" asked
Little Toot, trembling,
his eyes clearing a bit
in the dark.
"I am a steamboat!"
said a gruff voice that
was deep and solemn.
"And so are my friends."

“*Steamboats!* But you don’t look like steamboats,” said Little Toot. “My Grandfather Toot said that steamboats were fire-eating monsters!”

COLONE

COLONEL

"Fire-eating monsters, are we!" snorted the steamboat. And Little Toot saw the name *Colonel* lettered in gold on his side.

The dignity of the *Colonel* was shaken. But after a moment his eyes lit up with pride. "Once it amounted to something to be a steamboat," he said, "back in those golden days on the river."

The *Colonel* smoked and
puffed and dreamed. "The
magnolias were in bloom,"
he went on, "and the sweet
scent of lilacs filled the
air as we steamed up to the
wharves of the great mansions."

Then the paddle-wheeler from
Paducah tried to churn up a bit of
excitement as he spoke, but
unfortunately he ran out of steam.

"Why, back in my day," he
wheezed, "I raced with the
fastest steamboats on the river—
with no less than the *Natchez*
and the *Rob't. E. Lee.*"

The most beautiful of all was the *River Queen*. All decked out in spun sugar and lace, she looked as delicious as a wedding cake. She sighed.

"We steamboats no longer have anywhere to go. There is nothing for us to do now," she said sadly. "Everyone has forgotten us."

The warmth of her smile engulfed Little Toot. Even in that dismal bayou the *River Queen* cast a spell of magic.

Suddenly the spell was
broken. Howls from the
wilderness grew louder.
The cries of the animals
became cries of distress.
The storm was invading
the bayou.
The Mississippi
had gone into flood!

Floodwaters poured into the bayou. Wave upon wave scooped up trees and stumps and pounded at the steamboats unmercifully.
All around there was a flapping of wings.
Shadowy forms of animals scurried about for safety, but is there any safe place in a flood?
"We must save the animals!" cried Little Toot.

Though try hard as they would,
the steamboats were too helpless
to move.
“We are done for,” they said.
Indeed, the old boats were about
ready to give up.

But Little Toot said, “No!”
With a gallant effort he
threw himself up and over
the floodwaters, tooting
for the steamboats to follow.

The old boats were amazed at his folly. It was a senseless thing to do. No one had ever won out against the might of the Mississippi in flood.

"Come on! Come on!" tooted the little tugboat. "Where is that pride of yours now?"

In the darkness a boiler began firing. Then another. And another. Soon there was a hissing of steam.

Quickly paddle wheels began to
splash and turn, and flames shot
out of tall chimneys, lighting
up all the bayou.

In no time at all the steamboats *were* like fiery monsters! They bounced and steamed over the floodwaters until their boilers almost burst.

COLONEL

Following Little Toot, they went into the deep, dark wilderness. Through wind and high water they rounded up all animals that had been stranded in the flood. The cries of the animals became soft, gentle murmurs.

When the old steamboats came out again, they were loaded from top deck to water line with muskrats, ’possums, raccoons, alligators, skunks, and squirrels.

COLONEL

The little coalboat was overjoyed
when he saw them come thrashing
their way out onto the river.

Bells rang. Calliopes purred their joyful tunes. And cheers went up from the people standing atop the levee.

It was a magnificent celebration! The steamboats were back again on the Mighty Mississippi. And once more the Old River was calm.

COLONEL

After the celebration, Little Toot
and the coalboat helped their
friends find a new home.

They found it—deep in a sunlit bayou. Life is filled with excitement for the animals now, and why shouldn't it be, when they have fire-eating monsters for friends?

COLONEL

Finally, it was time for Little Toot to leave. "I hate to go," he told his friend the coalboat, "but I've been away from home too long.

"Besides," he added with a twinkle, "I've got a story to tell about the Mississippi River my Grandfather Toot won't believe."

*The Author*

HARDIE GRAMATKY is the author-illustrator of the children's classic, *Little Toot*. For a third of a century children have delighted in the adventures of the pixie-ish tugboat. Three sequels have told of the further adventures of Little Toot, while eight other books for children have come from the author's colorful imagination. Mr. Gramatky is famous for his paintings and is the winner of more than forty major awards for watercolors.